T H E
Veterans Day
Celebrations

Beauty in Books

The Veterans Day Celebration:
A Patriotic Journey

ISBN: 978-1-961634-32-9

Chapter 1: A Special Event

As the vibrant autumn colors started to bloom, Sophie's dad, who was reading the paper, suddenly looked up from his paper and told Max and Sophie about a unique Veterans Day Celebration story to honor the brave men and women who served their country and the opportunity for anyone to participate in the celebrations.

Max and Sophie happily decided that they would like to participate in the Veteran's day Celebrations with hearts bubbling with joy and anticipation.

Two days later, Max and Sophie arrived at the Veterans Memorial on the day of the celebration, a place filled with memories of remembrance and gratitude.

Chapter 2: Exploring the Veterans Memorial

They eagerly walked among the statues and read the names of the heroes who had sacrificed their lives for their freedom. Their hearts filled with awe, and they yearned to learn more about these courageous individuals.

Chapter 3: The Forgotten Medal

While exploring the memorial, Sophie stumbled upon a forgotten medal hidden in the grass. Intrigued, she and Max realized it was a symbol of great courage and bravery. They both knew they had to find the medal's owner and get to the bottom of the story behind it.

Chapter 4: Honoring Heroes

As Sophie and Max followed the clues, they visited local veterans' organizations, listened to inspiring stories, and met real-life heroes. They learned about the sacrifices made by veterans and how their service shaped the nation.

Chapter 5: The Puzzle Unfolds

The clues led Max and Sophie to historical landmarks. From a war memorial in the town square to a preserved battlefield site, they pieced together the puzzle, uncovering stories of bravery, resilience, and sacrifice.

VETERANS

Chapter 6: A Tribute to Service

In their quest, Max and Sophie organized a special event for veterans in the community. They gathered their friends, families, and neighbors to express appreciation and gratitude. They honored the veterans.' service and sacrifice through heartfelt speeches, music, and art.

Chapter 7: A Surprise Reunion

As they almost finished the puzzle, Max and Sophie received a surprise visit from the medal's owner. A decorated veteran, now aged but still proud, shared his experiences and thanked them for their efforts. It was a touching moment that left a lasting impact on their hearts.

Chapter 8: Forever Grateful

Max and Sophie felt fulfilled after finishing the puzzle and returning the medal. They learned that Veterans Day is an opportunity to express gratitude and remember those who fought for freedom. They decided to carry the spirit of honor and appreciation throughout their lives.

Epilogue: The Journey Continues

As Veterans Day celebrations ended, Max and Sophie sat on a park bench, their hearts filled with gratitude and respect for the brave men and women who had served their country. The Veterans Day Quest had left an indelible mark on their souls, creating a deep appreciation for the sacrifices made by men and women in uniform.

Max and Sophie knew they had a responsibility to honor the spirit of Veterans Day throughout the year. They promised to support veterans and their families and help whenever possible. They participated in ceremonies, laying wreaths on the graves of fallen heroes, their hearts swelling with pride and reverence.

The End

Check out my other books by
Scanning the QR code or using
the link below

linktr.ee/beautyinbooks3

About the Author

"Aby Sparklewood is an accomplished author with a unique talent for crafting captivating children's fiction and insightful business books. With a playful imagination and a keen business sense, her stories ignite young minds and inspire entrepreneurs to reach new heights of success."